Bobbo Goes to School

For Clare Hall-Craggs and family

Some other books by Shirley Hughes:

Alfie Gets in First
Alfie's Feet
Alfie Gives a Hand
An Evening at Alfie's
Alfie and the Birthday Surprise
Alfie Wins a Prize
Alfie and the Big Boys
All About Alfie
Don't Want to Go!
Dogger

BOBBO GOES TO SCHOOL
A BODLEY HEAD BOOK 978 0 370 33207 9

Published in Great Britain by The Bodley Head, an imprint of Random House Children's Books
A Random House Group Company
This edition published 2012

1 3 5 7 9 10 8 6 4 2

RANDOM HOUSE CHILDREN'S BOOKS
61–63 Uxbridge Road, London W5 5SA

www.**kidsatrandomhouse**.co.uk
www.**randomhouse**.co.uk

Addresses for companies within The Random House Group Limited can be found at:
www.randomhouse.co.uk/offices.htm

THE RANDOM HOUSE GROUP Limited Reg. No. 954009
A CIP catalogue record for this book is available from the British Library.

Printed in China

The Random House Group Limited supports the Forest Stewardship Council (FSC®),
the leading international forest certification organization. Our books carrying the FSC label are printed on
FSC®-certified paper. FSC is the only forest certification scheme endorsed by the leading environmental organizations,
including Greenpeace. Our paper procurement policy can be found at www.randomhouse.co.uk/environment.

MIX
Paper from
responsible sources
FSC® C020056

Bobbo Goes to School

Shirley Hughes

THE BODLEY HEAD

LONDON

It was Monday morning and Mum was loading the washing machine. Lily wasn't helping. She was hiding Bobbo amongst the towels and sheets.

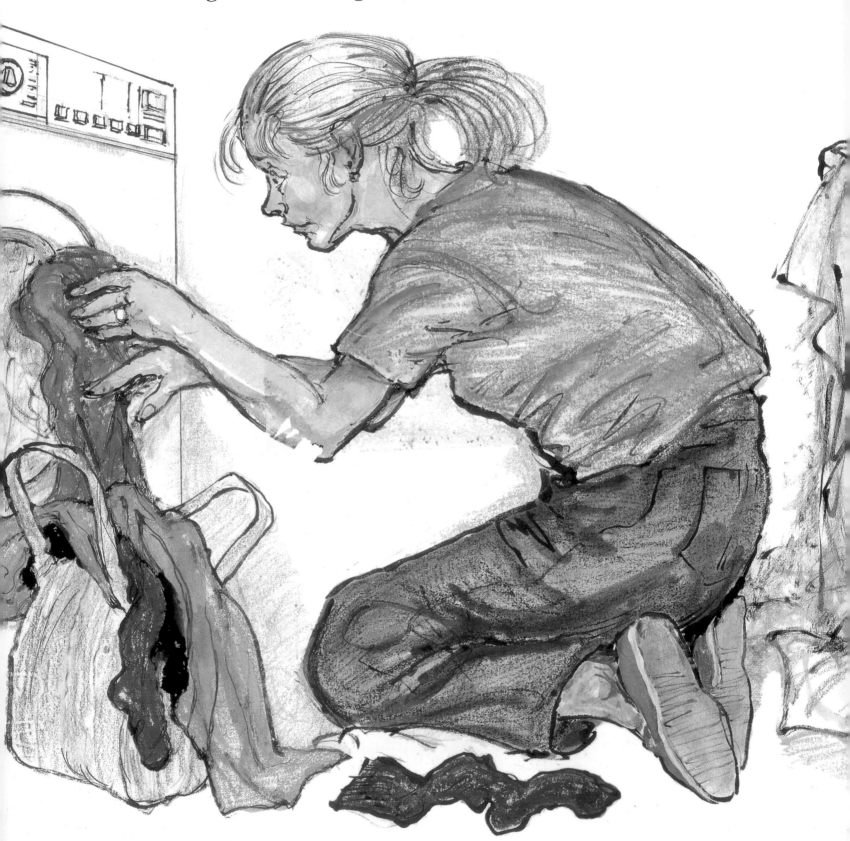

"Oh, do stop that, Lily," said Mum, "or I'll never get this done."

Lily stopped. But then she started to throw Bobbo into the air and catch him by the leg. Bobbo could tell it was going to be one of Lily's bad days.

After Mum had turned on the washing machine it was
time to go shopping. She pulled Lily's sweater
over her head and pushed her arms into
the sleeves. Lily did not help. She went
all limp like a rag doll.

"Shall we take Bobbo?"
said Mum. "I'm sure
he'd like to come."

Lily stopped going
limp, and together
they looked for Bobbo.
They found him hiding
under a cushion. At last
they were ready to set off.

While Lily and Bobbo were waiting on the pavement for Mum to open up the buggy, they saw the school bus draw up.

The driver got out and helped the school children to jump on board. Then he got in again and started the engine.

Just as the bus was pulling away, Lily did a dreadful thing. She swung Bobbo round and round by his leg and threw him high into the air – just like that! Bobbo flew up head first and landed smack on the roof of the bus, just as it was pulling out into the traffic.

Lily and Mum were too shocked
to move. They both stood there
and watched as the bus gained
speed and disappeared.

"Bobbo! I want him back!"
wailed Lily.

But it was too late. Bobbo
was gone.

Lily and Mum rushed back indoors and Mum got on the phone straight away. She spoke to the lady at the school and told her that Bobbo would soon be arriving on top of the school bus and would they please rescue him.

Lily cried and cried. "He might fall off and get run over!" she howled. "And I won't see him again ever!"

In fact Bobbo had not fallen off. He was lying face up, rushing along very fast and looking up at the sky. Sometimes he slipped a bit, but he stayed on board. This was all rather exciting for Bobbo. He had never travelled on a bus without Lily before.

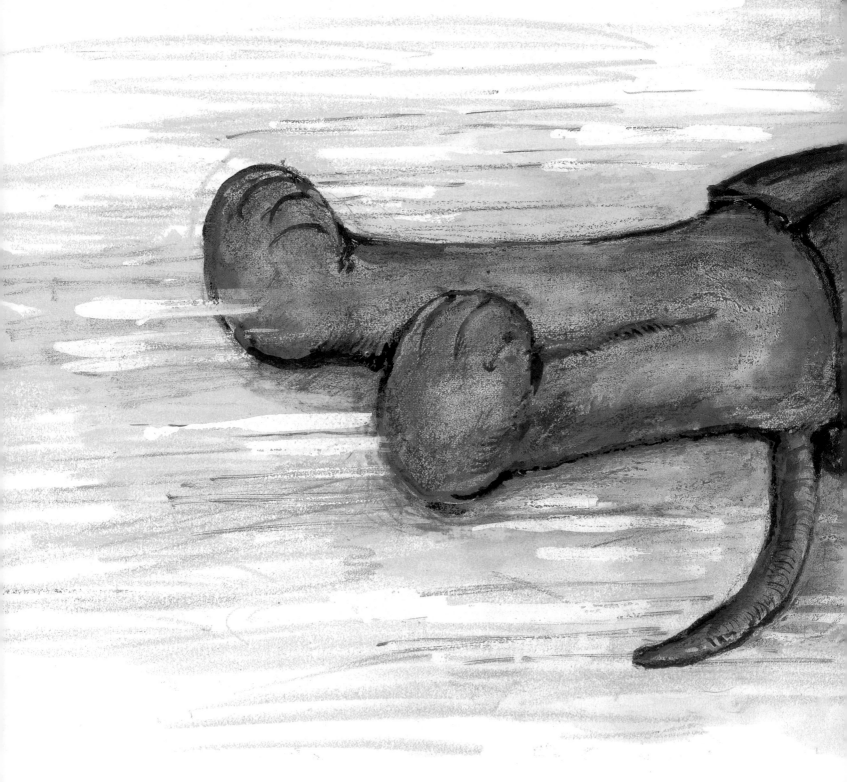

Down below the children laughed and chatted and looked out of the bus window. They would never have imagined that Bobbo was riding on the roof of their bus.

Soon they arrived at the school. The driver pulled up near the entrance doors, and that sent Bobbo straight into a bush.

It felt like being a bird. For a moment he thought he *was* a bird. He felt rather tired after all this excitement, so he just lay there, swaying gently and wondering what would happen next.

What an extraordinary day this was turning out to be for Bobbo!

Back at home Lily's day was
going from bad to worse. Mum
telephoned the school again.

But the lady who answered
said that the driver had looked
on top of the bus and no soft
toy had been found there.

Lily wept. It was terrible to think
that she had thrown away her
oldest, dearest friend.

"I want Bobbo back *now*!"
she sobbed.

Meanwhile, as Bobbo was resting among the leaves,
the school children came out to play.

A little girl called Natasha, who was playing under the bush with her friend, found Bobbo and handed him to the teacher.

All the children crowded round and made a great fuss of him. No one knew where he had come from.

So they took him to their classroom and put him in a special place on the Interest Shelf where he could see everything.

He sat there for the rest of the morning while the children did counting and drew pictures and listened to a story.

When the lady in the school office heard that Bobbo had been found, she telephoned Mum and Lily and they drove to the school straight away. Lily was allowed to go into the classroom to collect him. When she saw him on the Interest Shelf, she ran straight over and hugged him tightly.

Then the teacher and children showed Lily what they
had been doing with Bobbo.

They told her that they had been playing a game: they were trying to guess what his name was. Each of them had written their guess down.

Lily told them that none of them had got it right because his name was Bobbo!
  She was very happy when she thanked them and said goodbye.

"Oh, what a relief that we've found him!" said Mum when at last they arrived back home. "I think he liked it at school, and you'll like it too, Lily, when you're old enough to go there."

Lily was hugging Bobbo very tightly, pressing her face against his nose. "I'll never, never throw you away again!" she whispered.

Bobbo said nothing.
Lily's bad day had turned out
well after all.